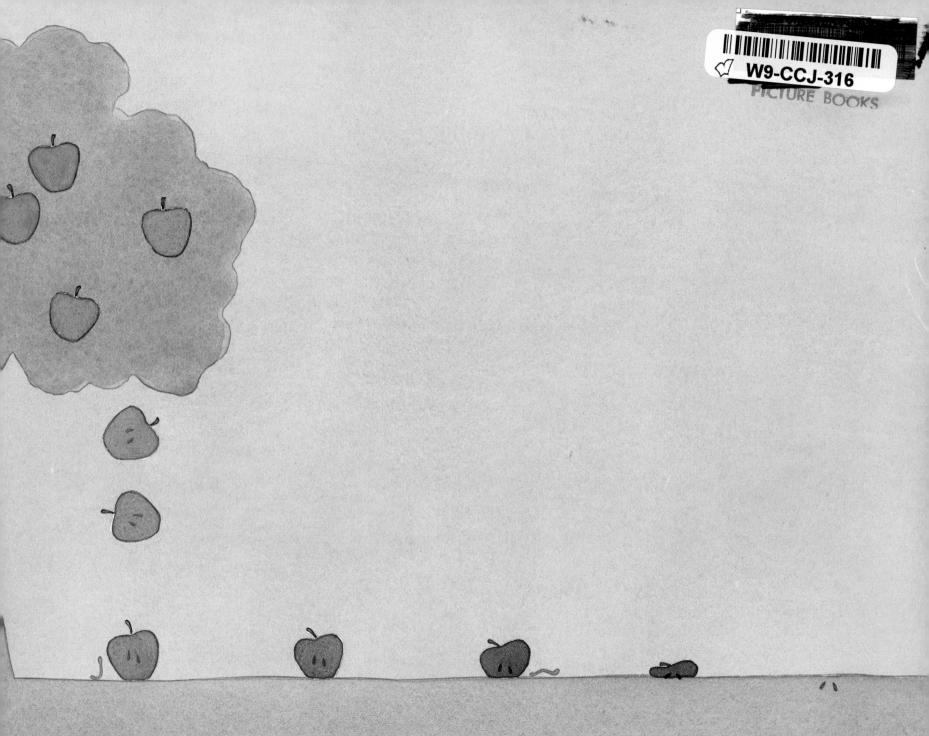

For my loving parents, Anita and David,
as well as my art teacher and friend, Jerry Sawitz

Many thanks to Ann Tobias

# Ned's New Home

## Kevin Tseng

**TRICYCLE PRESS**
Berkeley / Toronto

Ned loved apple pie,
and his favorite color had always been red,
so living in an apple was wonderful . . .

until the apple started to rot.

The walls turned to mush,
and apple juice rained every day.

When the bathtub began to float, Ned knew
it was time to look for a new home.

First he found a pear. It was
about the same size as his old house . . .

but the pear was too wobbly,
and Ned kept tumbling out.

Humph!

A watermelon was sturdier...

and **BIGGER**—much too big for little Ned.

Next, he built a house with blueberries . . .

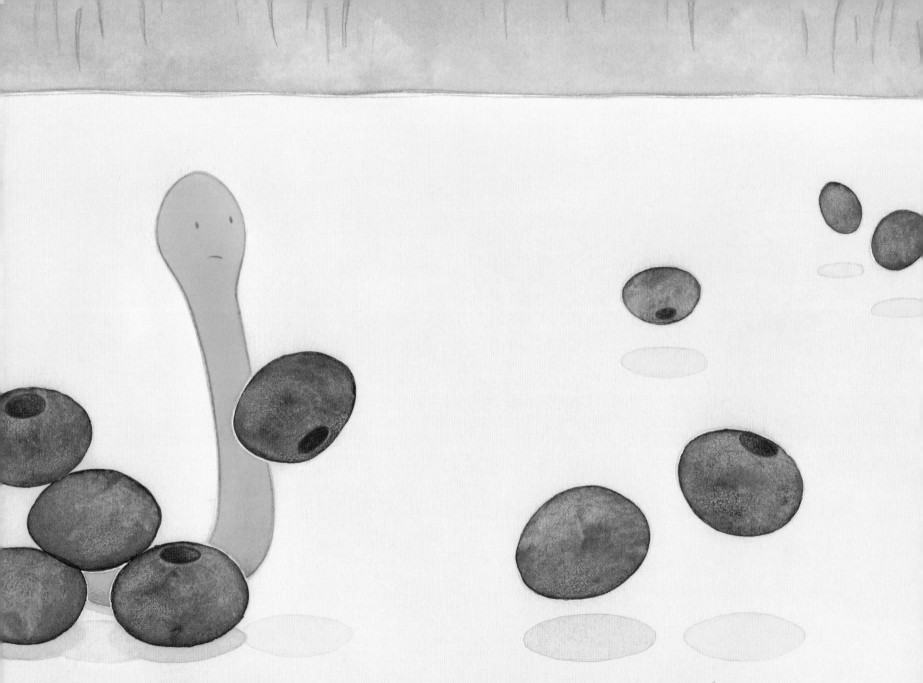

but when he tried to move in, they all rolled away.

Ned liked yellow almost as much as red,
so he was happy to live in a lemon . . .

until his friends tasted his sour lemon tarts.

And though a kiwi was sweet...

So, Ned found a bowl of bright red cherries.
He was planning a new house, when suddenly . . .

Up, up he went, higher and higher!
This was no place for a worm.

Ned jumped from the cherry
and gently floated down . . .

Whew!

landing in a tree full of big, beautiful . . .

apples!

Ned had found his perfect new home. The shape, the size, and the color were all just right—and it was delicious.

Ned baked an apple pie
almost every day for his old friends . . .

Mmm.

and made a disguise
to wear with his new friend.

TRICYCLE PRESS
*an imprint of Ten Speed Press*
PO Box 7123
Berkeley, California 94707
www.tricyclepress.com

Design by Betsy Stromberg
Typeset in Helvetica Rounded
The illustrations in this book were rendered in watercolor.

Library of Congress Cataloging-in-Publication Data

Tseng, Kevin, 1973–
  Ned's new home / Kevin Tseng.
      p. cm.
  Summary: A worm tries out a variety of new homes when the apple he
has been living in starts to rot, but none—from a lemon to a watermelon—
is satisfactory.
  ISBN-13: 978-1-58246-297-4 (hardcover)
  ISBN-10: 1-58246-297-6 (hardcover)
 [1. Worms—Fiction. 2. Fruit—Fiction. 3. Dwellings—Fiction.
4. Home—Fiction.]  I. Title.
  PZ7.T7872Ne 2009
  [E]—dc22
                    2008042385


First Tricycle Press printing, 2009
Printed in China

1 2 3 4 5 6 — 13 12 11 10 09